JE READER

Dear Parent:

Congratulations! Your child is taking the first steps on an exciting journey. The destination? Independent reading!

STEP INTO READING® will help your child get there. The program offers five steps to reading success. Each step includes fun stories and colorful art. There are also Step into Reading Sticker Books, Step into Reading Math Readers, Step into Reading Write-In Readers, Step into Reading Phonics Readers, and Step into Reading Phonics First Steps! Boxed Sets—a complete literacy program with something for every child.

Learning to Read, Step by Step!

Ready to Read Preschool–Kindergarten
• big type and easy words • rhyme and rhythm • picture clues
For children who know the alphabet and are eager to begin reading.

Reading with Help Preschool–Grade 1
• basic vocabulary • short sentences • simple stories
For children who recognize familiar words and sound out new words with help.

Reading on Your Own Grades 1–3
• engaging characters • easy-to-follow plots • popular topics
For children who are ready to read on their own.

Reading Paragraphs Grades 2–3
• challenging vocabulary • short paragraphs • exciting stories
For newly independent readers who read simple sentences with confidence.

Ready for Chapters Grades 2–4
• chapters • longer paragraphs • full-color art
For children who want to take the plunge into chapter books but still like colorful pictures.

STEP INTO READING® is designed to give every child a successful reading experience. The grade levels are only guides. Children can progress through the steps at their own speed, developing confidence in their reading, no matter what their grade.

Remember, a lifetime love of reading starts with a single step!

SEP 0 3 2008

Special thanks to Rob Hudnut, Shelley Dvi-Vardhana, Vicki Jaeger, Monica Okazaki,
Christine Chang, Jennifer Twiner McCarron, Shawn McCorkindale, Pat Link, Tulin Ulkutay,
and Ayse Ulkutay

Visit us on the Web!
www.stepintoreading.com
www.barbie.com

Educators and librarians, for a variety of teaching tools, visit us at
www.randomhouse.com/teachers
Library of Congress Cataloging-in-Publication Data
Depken, Kristen L.
Barbie & the Diamond Castle / adapted by Kristen L. Depken ; based on the original screenplay by
Cliff Ruby & Elana Lesser. — 1st ed.
    p. cm.
ISBN 978-0-375-85619-8 (trade) — ISBN 978-0-375-95619-5 (lib. bdg.)
I. Ruby, Cliff. II. Lesser, Elana. III. Barbie and the Diamond Castle (motion picture) IV. Title. V. Title:
Barbie and the Diamond Castle.
PZ8.D4383Bar 2008
[E]—dc22
2008011531

Printed in the United States of America   10 9 8 7 6 5 4 3 2 1   First Edition

Adapted by Kristen L. Depken

Based on the original screenplay
by Cliff Ruby & Elana Lesser

Illustrations by
Ulkutay Design Group & Allan Choi

Random House 🏠 New York

Alexa and Liana
are best friends.
They love to sing.
One day,
they find magic stones.
They make necklaces.
They promise to be
best friends always.

Later that day,
Liana and Alexa meet
a poor old woman.

The girls give her
their lunch.
The woman gives them
an old mirror.

At home,

the girls sing.

A third voice joins in.

It is coming

from the mirror!

A girl named Melody

is trapped inside.

Melody tells the story
of the Diamond Castle.
Three muses lived there.
But evil Lydia wanted
to be the only muse.

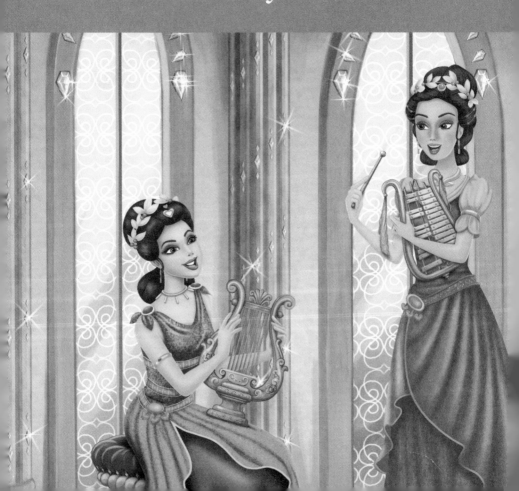

The two good muses
hid the Diamond Castle.
They gave Melody the key.
Then Lydia turned
the good muses to stone.

Now Lydia wants the key
to the Diamond Castle.
Lydia's dragon, Slyder,
must find Melody.

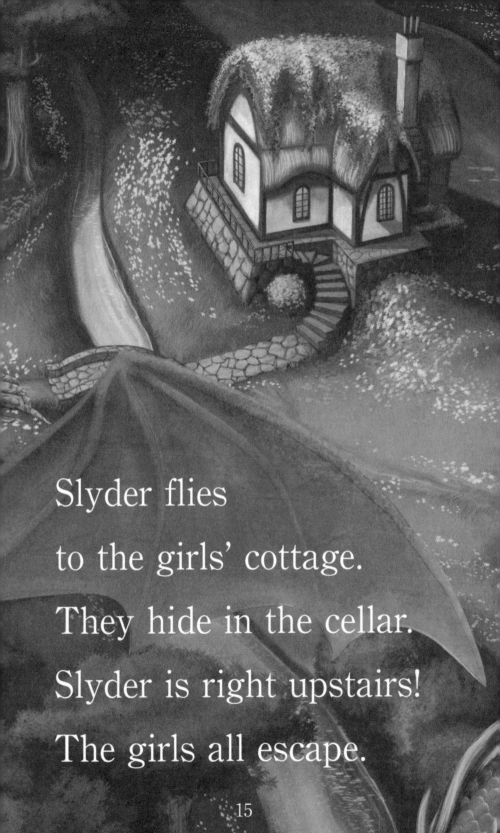

Slyder flies
to the girls' cottage.
They hide in the cellar.
Slyder is right upstairs!
The girls all escape.

Melody still has the key.
She can save the muses.
Alexa and Liana
set out for the castle
with the mirror.

On the way,
they find two puppies.
They name them
Lily and Sparkles.

Soon the girls
meet twin brothers.

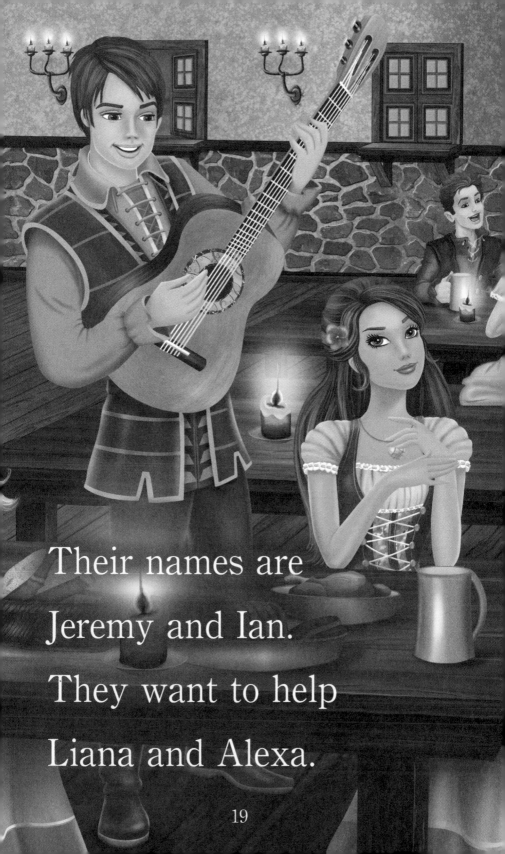

Their names are
Jeremy and Ian.
They want to help
Liana and Alexa.

Lydia and Slyder look
for Alexa and Liana.
Slyder chases them!

The twins rescue
the girls just in time!

Alexa and Liana
rest at a manor.
They find food to eat
and they try on gowns.

But the girls argue.

Alexa wants to stay.

Liana thinks
they should keep going.

Lydia lures both girls
to her cavern.
She puts Alexa
under a spell.

Alexa is
going to fall!
Liana and Lily
save her.
The girls are
friends again.

Now Lydia has
the mirror.
Melody is still inside!
Lydia creates
a whirlpool.

She uses a spell
to make the girls
walk into it.
But they trick her!

Alexa grabs
Lydia's magic flute.
Liana saves the mirror
from Lydia.

Alexa and Liana sing.
Then the Diamond
Castle appears!
Singing was the key!

Melody appears, too.
She is free
from the mirror!
The Diamond Castle
sparkles with magic.

Lydia and Slyder

turn to stone.

The good muses are free.

Liana and Alexa become
Princesses of Music.
Their gowns sparkle.
Liana, Alexa,
and Melody are
best friends always.